Published by Parkhurst Brothers Publishers, PO Box 356, Marion, Michigan 49665.
Distributed by Chicago Distribution Center: 800-621-2736.
Trade orders welcome through major distributors.
Publicity contact: ted@parkhurstbrothers.com or 231-215-0488.

Printed in the United States of America.

Illustration by Brian Lei

Cover and Interior design by Brian Lei, Nancy Wang & Robert Kikuchi-Yngojo

Typography: Goudy OldStyle

This publication made possible, in part, by support from
**Eth-Noh-Tec**
977 South Van Ness Avenue,
San Francisco, CA 94110

We recommend these resources on the web:
ethnohtec.org
parkhurstbrothers.com
storynet.org

# A New Pair of Wings

Written by
Nancy Wang & Robert Kikuchi-Yngojo

Illustrated by
Brian Lei

This book is dedicated to mother,
**Delores Yngojo Kikuchi**

**Parkhurst Brothers Publishers**
M A R I O N ,   M I C H I G A N

"Tell me my favorite story, Mama! Pleeease!!" begged little Delores.

But Mama Tacion warned, "It is past your bedtime. Remember, tomorrow is a big day! We leave our little village and go all the way to America to be with Papa!"

"All the more reason, Mama. Tell me one more time. It's our last night in the Philippines. Pleeease?"

Mama Tacion smiled. "All right little Delores. Now close your eyes."

"*No'ong u'nang panahon*, once upon a time, a long time ago, there were Seven Star Maidens up in the Heavenly Skyworld...

Swoosh! Seven Maidens flying from the Sky World down to Earth to swim in their favorite secret mountain pool.

Splash! Seven lovely maidens in their beautiful fairy gowns of orange and black."

"Mama, I can see them!! They are real!"

"Ah, but soon, little Delores, it was time for them to go to the sky world. So they turned three times round and round, and up up they flew back to the stars."

3

"Mama, they are REAL,"
murmured little Delores as she fell asleep.

That night, she had a dream that before the
Star Maidens flew away, they gave her a magic charm.
They told her as long as she treasured it, she could fly back
and forth between two worlds, the Sky World and Earth.

"Like us," whispered the maidens. "We will place it in the banana trees so
no one else but you can find it! Use it whenever you want to ....flyyyyy!!"

Suddenly, "*Inday*, dear one, time to get up!"

"Mama, the Star Maidens gave me a magic charm!"

"Magic charm?"

Delores ran out of the house and into the banana grove.

"*Ano?* What is that?"

Delores saw something tiny and green hanging from
a banana leaf. Almost shiny. Not wood. Not metal.
Very still. Just dangling under the banana leaf.

"Is this my magic charm?"

She was about to reach out and touch it when…

"Delores! Come!" and Mama Tacion
grabbed her by the hand.

"But Mama, my magic charm!"

8

After two boats to two islands, finally they were standing upon the deck of a very large ship steaming across the gigantic Pacific Ocean.

"CLANG CLANG! BOOOO-AAAAH!
BOOOO-AAAAH! CLANG CLANG!"

"Look at all the stars, Mama! I'm looking for the Star Maidens.
They have to give me my magic charm in America now."

Finally the ship arrived in San Francisco!
Suddenly, through the crowds of big people and big noises,
a pair of big hands lifted little Delores into the air!

"I'm flying!"

It was Rafael Yngojo, her proud papa,
whom she was meeting for the very first time!

"*Inday!* Dear one! Delores!
You are so *maganda*, beautiful!

Welcome to America! Come!
Let's go to your new home!"

Delores climbed up into a big car.
As she looked out the window, she
saw so many big houses whiz by.
Soon she was climbing stairs into a
very big building!

How different than her bamboo and
nipa palm hut in the Philippines.

Before long, "Delores, time to eat!
Your favorite! Chicken Adobo stew."

"But Mama, where are the stars
in San Francisco?"

An evening fog had rolled
across the City. How could
the Star Maidens find her?

She would have to find them.
But, she needed the Magic Charm
so she could put on her new wings.

"Delores! It's delicious ... *Masarap!*"
called her Papa. "*Ka-on, na.* eat
now. You have to go to bed soon.
Tomorrow is your first day of school!"

"School?! New friends!" and Delores
forgot all about her magic charm and
the Star Maidens.

The next morning, the household was a bustle of activity!

Here is your lunch!" said Mama Tacion as she handed
Delores a bag with a banana and a container of
left-over rice and chicken adobo.

"Be a good girl, Delores," said Papa.

"I will. I'm going to make
some new friends today!"

13

Once inside the classroom, Delores smiled at her classmates.
In the sing-song tones of her Ilongo Filipino language,
she greeted them, "*Kumasta ka*? How are you?"

But, all the other children just giggled.

Delores politely asked again, *"Kumasta ka? How are you?"*

This time the children pointed at Delores and laughed out loud.

"Children, that's enough! Delores, English is not so hard. Watch me."

The teacher began to move her hands to form pictures,

"Book… Cook … Look."

"Buuuk … Kook … Luke."

The children giggled again.

Now Delores was afraid
to speak at all.

"Oh Star Maidens, where are you?
I don't like it here. They make fun of me.
I wish I could fly back home to the Philippines.
Is that where you are? I need my magic charm.
I need my new wings. I want to go back to our *real* home."

But no matter how hard she wished to be back home in the Philippines, she was still in America. She didn't have her magic charm. She didn't have her new wings.

Then one day, Delores' teacher brought a glass jar to school and placed it on her desk. All the children gathered around to look.

The jar didn't have pickles in it.

The jar didn't have mayonnaise in it.

The jar didn't have candy in it.

The jar had a twig and some small leaves.

And something else!

...something tiny and green hanging from the very top leaf.

Almost shiny. Not wood. Not metal. Very still.

Just dangling under the leaf.

"My magic charm from the Star Maidens!" cried out Delores in her sing-song language. "How did the teacher get it?"

"Buuuk … Kook … Luke! Look!"

"Teacher! Delores spoke English!"

"Buuuk ... Kook … Luke … LOOK!"

That something hanging under the leaf began to wiggle and squiggle!

"LOOK! LOOK! LOOK!" everyone shouted.

That something hanging under the leaf began to open!

" Look! It's a Star Maiden in her black and orange gown!" shouted Delores as she slipped back into her Ilongo Filipino language.

But, this time, no one teased her.
Everyone was staring at the wiggling miracle.

The creature's gown curled open, curled wider, stretching into two beautiful orange and black wings.

"*Alibangbang!*" cried out little Delores. "*Alibangbang!*"

"Butterfly!" screamed the children.

BUT-TER-FFLLLYYY!" Delores repeated. "*Alibangbang!*" she added.

"*ALIBANGBANG!*" her classmates echoed.

"BUTTERFLYYY! *ALIBANGBANG!*" shouted the children.

Delores began waving her arms up and down.
"BUTTERFLYYY! *ALIBANGBANG!*"

All the other children waved their arms, too!

And as Delores began to dance around and around the classroom,
all her new friends followed, shouting and giggling,

"BUTTERFLYYY! *ALIBANGBANG!*

BUTTERFLYYY! *ALIBANGBANG!*"

That night, gazing up at the stars from her bedroom window,
little Delores could feel her heart swell with joy.

"Was that you today at my school? *Maraming salamat!*
Thank you! Thank you for my magic charm."

Delores now knew that she would always be able to fly
between her two worlds, between her two languages.

She stretched, turned three times,
spread her arms out wide and flew to bed.

In this way, little Delores got her new pair of wings.

Tomorrow would be a great day! She was home in America.

## About Delores Yngojo Kikuchi:

Delores grew up in San Francisco and became a nurse. She married Dr. John Kikuchi and moved to Concord, California where she was an active member of the Concord, CA Friends of the Library and often developed displays of Filipino culture. She founded the Filipino Folk Dance Club of Contra Costa; co-founded The Filipino American Club in Concord, CA with her husband and friends. She had 5 children and played the piano as her husband sang. In her senior years, she took a writing class and submitted a poem of her immigration, which won first place in a writing contest. She passed this story on to storytellers/authors Robert (son) and Nancy (daughter-in-law) who celebrate the messages of diversity and compassion by performing stories all over the world.

## About the Authors:

Nancy Wang and Robert Kikuchi-Yngojo live in San Francisco, CA and began their career as storytellers in 1987. They founded Eth-Noh-Tec, their Asian American story performance non-profit in 1981 and have traveled the world performing their unique style of telling, weaving movement and music with the spoken word. They have two grown children.
*www.ethnohtec.org*

Photo by Leon Sun.

## About the Illustrator:

Brian Lei is an artist and illustrator living in San Francisco. His mission is to create art that matters. One of the ultimate goals he has is to change the world on how it interacts with art. He also plans to become the best in his field like the old masters he admires.
*www.brianlei.com*